THE FINAL SOLUTION

BASED ON HUGH HOWEY'S HALF WAY HOME UNIVERSE

COLONY COLLAPSE

BOOK 1

ROZ MARSHALL

Find out more about the author and upcoming books online at
www.rozmarshall.co.uk/books

Get **a FREE short story**—sign up for my newsletter:
rozmarshall.co.uk/newsletter/

CONTENTS_

ABOUT THIS STORY_

There's a solution. But it's not the one they anticipated.

They started with five hundred, but their numbers are decreasing every day. Exponentially.

Science Officer Brent and Medical Officer Kelley are tasked with discovering who—or what—is picking off colonists from their expeditionary settlement on the seeming Eden of this alien planet.

But science and logic are no match for their rapacious nemesis, as they race to find a solution before their colony becomes unviable and the unthinkable becomes reality.

FOREWORD_

This story is set in **Hugh Howey**'s *Half Way Home* universe, telling the story of another colony on a different planet. I would like to thank Hugh for his amazing generosity in letting us use our imaginations to play in his fictitious universe.

CHAPTER ONE_

On the third day we found the first body.

At the time, Colony, our guiding AI, didn't seem particularly concerned— *"One body is an aberration, not a pattern,"* it said—but Kelley, our Medical Officer, insisted on taking the remains for a post-mortem.

Personally, I thought she was just looking for some practice, since it was only three days since we'd been birthed from the amniotic vats where we'd been grown from cloned blastocysts, emerging as fully formed and fully-trained thirty year-olds. But as Science Officer, I had some professional interest in what she found, so I gave her a couple of hours, then made my way to the hospital module.

"It's a strange one, Brent," she said, looking at me through the plastic face mask.

The body on the stainless steel table was partially covered by a thin rubber sheet, but the head and shoulders were exposed. I peered down at it, confused by what I was seeing. "Do we know who he was?"

"Gregor 489. Kitchen porter, I believe. The working hypothesis is that he was collecting water from the stream when—" she paused, and frowned, "something happened."

"No theories yet as to who killed him, then?"

"Sadly, no. As you can see," she gestured at the exposed skin, "he's very desiccated already, and it's made identifying any injury sites very difficult."

From her expression, I could see that there was something she wasn't telling me. "But—?" I asked.

Taking off the mask, she walked to the side of the room and picked up a water bottle, then propped herself against the bench and cradled the bottle. "It's weird." She tapped a forefinger on her lower lip. "Usually, gravity pools the blood at the lowest point of a dead body."

"I've heard of that. Lividity?"

"Yes, lividity." She was biting her thumbnail now, and staring at nothing.

I walked over and propped myself beside her. "And?" I raised my eyebrows, encouraging her to continue.

"This body has no lividity." She looked sideways at me. "In fact, it has no blood at all."

————

Crosby looked over the table at us, bushy eyebrows scrunched together. "When it was just Gregor, I didn't think too much about it—assumed he'd drunk the water without boiling it first, or somesuch. But this morning we found two more bodies, and it's looking like security needs to get involved."

"So we'd like your input," continued Luc, our commanding officer, looking from me to Kelley. "You saw the first body yesterday; we'd like you to examine these two in situ, and see if there's anything in the location that jumps out at you."

"Not literally, I hope!" joked Kelley.

But Crosby took her seriously. "We'll have a Security Officer go with you, just in case."

————

"WHO WERE THEY?" I ASKED, LOOKING DOWN at the sad scene. Obviously, these two had already started to fulfil one of our objectives—to pair off, recreate and build a community—but their union had been short-lived. I looked across at Kelley and found myself wondering whether our cloned bodies and identical genetics meant that the same pairs formed on *every* planet colonised by our masters from Earth.

The security officer shrugged. "Eli 431 and Tori 278, so I'm told."

I raised my eyebrows. With a number like that, Tori had been a relatively high-caste female, so Eli had done well to pair off with her. Not that it had done him much good.

Kelley squatted beside the bodies, peering closely at any skin that was exposed to the air.

Leaving her with the medical examination, I looked around me. We were standing under a tree by one of the farms, near the electric fence that surrounded our compound. This fence acted as a barrier to any alien wildlife or beings that might have ill intentions towards five hundred young colonists sent from far-away Earth to populate and exploit the planet on behalf of mission sponsors they'd never even met. So it *should* have kept out any potential killers that were native to planet Kc98934.

But this planet had been chosen by our AI precisely because it had not yet evolved animal life more complex than invertebrates. I turned my gaze towards the collection of modules around our central command pod, wondering if, instead, there was something faulty in the genetics of one of my colleagues which had turned them into a killer?

———

ARRANGING A SLIDE OF DIRT FROM THE murder site under my microscope, I motioned my Lab Assistant, Dina, to join me. "Could you do me a favour, and get me a beaker of water from the stream where they found Gregor?"

"Yes boss," she said, and headed out of the Clean Room into the main lab.

Once she'd gone, I concentrated on what I was seeing through the magnifier lenses. Which was nothing out of the ordinary, unfortunately. Straightening up, I sighed, stretching my arms and resting them on my head as I contemplated this case. So far, the science wasn't telling me anything.

Perhaps it was time to see if the medical evidence was any more enlightening.

———

Kelley looked up as I entered her lab, and I could tell from her expression that her luck had been better than mine.

My raised eyebrows asked the question.

"It's a strange one. These guys—" she motioned at the bodies lying on the shiny surface, "were found more quickly than Gregor, and yet they're still very desiccated."

"And bloodless?" I asked.

"Yes," she nodded. "But they're not quite as bad as Gregor was."

"So it might be something to do with the atmosphere of the planet that accelerates the decomposition?"

"Perhaps. But the blood loss would probably explain most of it, to be honest." She pointed back at the table. "I haven't told you about the most interesting finding, though." Walking to the examination bench, she lifted the rubber sheet from Tori's foot, and motioned me over. "Look."

I leaned over, and saw what she was pointing

at. There was some sort of injury on the pale, leathery skin of Tori's inner ankle, like a circular bruise. "Could she have done that by accident?" I asked.

"Maybe—except that he has one too, but this time on his wrist."

It was the first clue we'd found, but it wasn't enough to explain these three mysterious deaths, and it wouldn't be enough to stop the next one.

CHAPTER TWO_

Back in my science lab, I examined the sample of farm dirt again, just in case I'd missed something the first time. But there really wasn't anything out of the ordinary to see. Perhaps there would be something more obvious in the water sample.

That thought made me look up. Where *was* Dina? She should've been back by now. Glancing at the clock on the wall, my mouth went dry, and I felt a trickle of fear ripple down my spine. How stupid was I? Caste number in single digits, and yet I'd sent her out on her own, with a killer on the loose.

Sprinting out of the door, I careened into Crosby, coming the other way.

"Crosby!" I grabbed his shoulders. "Dina? Have you seen her?"

"Just passed her heading into the mess tent." My face must've shown my relief, as he added, "What's up?"

I grimaced. "She went off for more samples; I started to get worried when she wasn't back." Then I realised that *he* had been on his way to *my* lab. "Were you looking for me? Have you found more evidence?"

Shaking his head, he said, "Unfortunately not. Another victim, I'm afraid."

———

LUC'S FACE WAS GRAVE. "THIS ONE WAS A FARM worker," he said. "One death was unfortunate, but four is starting to look positively careless. Colony is giving me a hard time. Do we have any leads yet?"

Lacing her fingers together, Kelley pursed her lips. "Not much to go on. All three bodies had been drained of blood, and the bodies of Tori and Eli both have a tiny circular mark, like a bruise."

"But not Gregor?" Crosby asked.

She shook her head. "His body was too desiccated to show a mark like that."

"See what you can find on this next victim, then," said Luc, staring earnestly across the table at us, "For our colony's sake, I need some answers about how they died." He turned to the security chief. "And, Crosby, we need to put some preventative measures in place—night-time security patrols; colonists to move about in pairs, not singly; and a curfew from dusk until dawn."

Crosby inclined his head. "Can I make a suggestion? I'd like to start questioning the colonists, to see if I can find anyone with a motivation for murder."

"Absolutely!" Pushing his chair back, Luc got up, signalling the meeting at an end, then turned back to us when he reached the door. "Guys, get me an answer on this. Find out who—or what—is killing our people. We can't afford to lose any more."

———

ON THE WAY BACK TO MY LAB, I STOPPED AT the mess tent to retrieve Dina and her sample.

"Sorry boss," she said, looking chastened. "My stomach reminded me that I'd missed lunch, so I popped in on my way past." She pointed at a table near the entrance. "The sample's over there." Taking a last bite of food, she followed me out of the tent.

But what we saw on the table stopped us short.

"I—It was full when I left it!" protested Dina, as we stared at the empty beaker. The bottom edge of the glass container had a circular hole in it, and all of the water had leaked out. There were still a few damp patches in evidence on the table's surface, but the hot atmosphere of this primeval planet had evaporated most of it.

Remembering Luc's directive, I scratched my chin. "We'll have to go get some more, then." Narrowing my eyes, I added, "*Together*, this time."

"Oh, I'm sorry, boss, I promise I'll come straight back this time, there's no need for you to come."

I shook my head. "Unfortunately there is. They've found another body, so there's a new security directive that we can only move about in pairs. Let's go back to the lab for a new container, and then head to the stream."

———

Passing the communications module, en route to the stream, we heard a piercing scream from somewhere near the centre of camp. Dina and I took one look at each other, and sprinted towards the sound.

When we reached the spot, Crosby was shouldering his way through the small crowd that had gathered. Crouching down, he glanced up at the nearest bystander. "Get the Doc. Now!"

"Can I help?" I asked, pushing through to the front, where I could see yet another body sprawled on the grass near the kitchens.

He looked up at me. "Get this lot out of the way, will you?"

People took the hint and started to walk away, whispering to each other. "He didn't mean you!" I put a hand on Dina's arm, just as Kelley arrived.

"Not *another* one," she said. "I've only just got the last body onto my examination table."

"Colony's going to be mad," said Crosby.

"*Luc*'s going to be mad," I added.

Crosby puffed out his cheeks. "Let's examine this scene quickly, and get some more samples." He glanced from Dina to me, and frowned. "Looks like you came prepared?"

"We were just on our way to get a sample from the stream," Dina said, before I had time to answer.

"Forget that for now, let's attend to this one." He shook his head. "Whoever the poor sod was."

———

WE LEARNED NOTHING NEW FROM THE BODIES of Kelvin 491 and Meria 399, but our colony was now missing a Farmer and a Sous-chef, and Crosby was getting twitchy. He insisted on sending a security officer with Dina and me when we finally got to make our trip to the stream.

"Is it true what they're saying around camp?" the dark-haired guard asked as we strode along the path in the fading light.

"What's that, Hickson?" I replied.

"That someone in the colony is— um— a vampire?"

Dina's gasp showed that she hadn't heard that story either.

"You should know better than to listen to rumours," I told him. But secretly, I'd been wondering the same thing.

———

HUNKERED BY THE STREAM, DINA AND I HAD our backs to Hickson when we heard a grunt, and spun around just in time to see him collapse, unconscious, to the ground.

I rushed to his side, motioning Dina to keep back. "Careful," I said. "Keep an eye out for trouble, will you?"

Feeling for his pulse, I gasped and jumped backwards.

I'd found the culprit.

Hooked onto his neck was a black, slug-like creature, which was growing rapidly in length as it sucked the life-blood from his body; writhing and wriggling in seeming ecstasy as it feasted on the rich red fluid in Hickson's arteries. But what I saw next made me recoil in horror.

CHAPTER THREE_

Striding around the table, my voice sounded unnatural to my ears. "It was like something out of a horror story!"

"Just sit down, and tell us what happened," Luc said, in a maddeningly calm voice.

But in my anxiety, I couldn't sit still. "So, the creature expanded, and then all of a sudden its tail broke off, and wriggled away, and then it happened again, and again, until one of them latched onto Dina's ankle." I stopped, and looked across at her white face. "Before I could think what I was doing, I'd knocked it off with my sample scoop, and then we ran for it."

"Did it bite you?" Kelley asked Dina.

She frowned, and looked down at her leg. "It

had just started to, when Brent knocked it off." A look of gratitude crossed her face as she gazed across at me.

"I think the slugs must inject some sort of anaesthetic when they first bite," I added. "She was pretty woozy and out of it on the way back. I had to prop her up to start with."

"We need to get you into hospital, young lady," said Kelley. "First of all, to check the wound just in case any part of the slug is still there, secondly to check there's no ill-effects from that anaesthetic, and thirdly to test your blood. You're the first victim who's actually had any blood left for me to test!"

———

After Kelley had taken Dina to the hospital, Luc turned to Crosby and me. "This is getting serious. Tonight, let's get section heads and essential staff to sleep in the modules, and keep everyone else in a tight circle of tents around the command area." He nodded at Crosby. "Get your officers working in shifts, patrolling the campsite."

"In pairs," added Crosby.

"Absolutely," agreed Luc.

Crosby cleared his throat, and opened his mouth as if to speak, but seemed to have a hard time finding the words.

"Is there something else?" asked Luc.

"I— uh, I wanted to ask your permission... I think it might be time to open the emergency weapons locker."

Luc stared at him for a moment, and then nodded curtly. "Yes, I think you're right. Arm the guards."

But, as we would discover, all the security in the world wouldn't be enough to stop those blood-thirsty alien creatures from satisfying their diabolical appetites.

———

We were woken at dawn by gunfire and panicked shouting.

Staggering outside in the half light, I could see a tousle-haired Kelley wearing an oversized t-shirt at the entry to the hospital across the way, the sleepy face of Dina peeking over her shoulder. The relief I felt at knowing that they were okay was a revelation to me. During our long apprenticeship in the vats, Colony AI had *taught* us about feelings and emotions, in the same way that it had taught me about logic and reason, but it wasn't until you actually encountered something in real life that the words transformed from theory into reality.

Running footsteps jolted me back to the present, and Crosby pelted round the side of the module. "Doc, Brent," he gasped, "management meeting—*now*. There's been more killings."

Pulling on a shirt and shoes, I pumped him for information. "What's happened? What were those gunshots?"

"That was one of my guards, trying to kill those — things. It's desperate out there. I— we—" He shook his head. "You can't imagine it."

At the main campsite area, we were met by a scene of confusion. The outer tents in disarray, a large crowd of colonists were huddled in the centre, looking lost and frightened.

Luc strode through the camp, seemingly oblivious to his own safety, and got their attention. "Colonists! I've posted guards on the mess tent; I'd like you all to go there now and eat breakfast, whilst the section heads and I hold a strategy meeting." His confidence had gained their attention, and some semblance of quiet fell over the group. "For now, all work is suspended, and we'll let you know how we're going to tackle this menace as soon as possible."

Catching my eye, Luc nodded towards Command, and I took the hint to head over for the meeting.

———

"WE'VE LOST OVER A HUNDRED IN JUST ONE night," said Crosby through a clenched jaw. "And five of those were my officers."

There was a ripple around the table as people absorbed this news.

"And what's more," he continued, "the slug numbers seem to be multiplying—it's like our blood is a catalyst, and every one that feeds makes five more."

Luc turned to me and Kelley. "Do we have any further scientific or medical insights into these creatures?"

I glanced at Kelley, then spoke first. "I did some reading last night, in the AI library. Although I called them slugs, they seem to share some characteristics with leeches—the blood-sucking and the proboscis." Seeing a couple of frowns, I translated. "The mouth sucker part. They're most active at night, and both species seem to prefer damp, humid places, so this jungle-like habitat is ideal for them."

Luc nodded slowly. "That makes sense. Most of the killings have been at night."

"And Meria was probably killed by a slug that escaped from Dina's stream sample," said Kelley.

"So how do people on Earth kill *their* slugs?" asked Crosby.

"Well, theirs aren't quite as deadly as ours," I said. "And they have natural predators—which seem to be missing here. On this planet, I think chemicals or fire—flame throwers—would be our best chance."

BUT FLAME-THROWERS DIDN'T WORK—SOMETHING in the slugs' slimy coating seemed to protect them from the flames—and nothing in our stores of chemicals seemed to have any effect on them. We'd already tried shooting them, but they just re-formed into multiple parts, and crushing them was useless, as they just morphed back into shape. Instead, all that we gained from our efforts to hunt and kill these seemingly-indestructible creatures was another three bodies to add to the growing list of colonists awaiting burial.

By the end of the day, we were no further forward in our fight against the vampiric molluscs, and with night approaching, everyone was starting to get nervous.

"Options?" Luc asked, as we sat in Command for another strategy meeting.

"I think we need to get everyone inside tonight," I said. "They're vulnerable out there in tents, but at least inside the modules we have the metal hulls to protect us."

"It'll be a squash to fit everyone in," said Milse, our Head of Ops, tapping a thumbnail against her teeth, "but I suppose it's better to be uncomfortable than dead."

"Okay, then make it happen, Milse," said Luc, and turned to our Head of Comms. "Nyota, I want you to send a priority one satellite message to Earth. Liaise with Brent for the wording to tell them about these creatures, and ask them if there's any science we've missed."

She nodded. "It'll take at least twelve hours for us to get an answer, though, by the time the message relays there and back."

Luc grimaced. "Okay." He stood up. "We'll reconvene at oh-seven-hundred tomorrow."

———

AFTER NYOTA HAD SENT THE MESSAGE TO Earth, Dina and I spent the rest of the evening in the Clean Room, sealed off from the rest of the lab and unsuccessfully trying to come up with some sort of chemical combination which might kill the slugs. When night fell, the rest of the module was full of nervous colonists, so we just laid out our bed rolls on the floor of the mini-lab and tried to get comfortable.

It took me some time to fall asleep, and, when I did, I had chaotic dreams of escaping through the jungle, pursued by some dark monster. Kelley was running with me in the dream, and she was screaming. At first I thought she was screaming at the monster, but then my foggy brain properly registered the messages from my ears, and I jerked awake, realising that the screaming was coming from beside me, in real life, not in a dream.

CHAPTER FOUR_

It seemed that not only could the slugs eat through glass, they could also eat through metal.

At some point during the night, they had found their way into the lab, and everyone inside it was dead; lying in funereal rows like shrivelled husks. The only survivors were the two of us in the sealed room.

Looking from the horrific scene on the lab floor back to the Clean Room door, Dina's eyes filled with tears. "I don't understand. How did *we* escape?"

My mouth and my brain didn't seem properly connected, but I managed to mumble, "Maybe they ran out of time before dawn?"

"Or perhaps the extra plastic cladding in the Clean Room made a difference?" suggested Dina.

Whatever it was, I felt guilty and wretched. If we hadn't kept working so late, perhaps some of the others would have been in there with us, and survived. And then my jumbled thoughts turned to the companion of my dream, and a fresh spasm of dread clawed at my stomach. "We need to go see if anyone else has made it," I said, and headed for the door.

———

OUTSIDE, EVERYTHING WAS SILENT. DEATHLY silent.

There were no sounds of people waking, or people sleeping, or people doing morning things. Just a bone-chilling stillness.

"Kelley!" I shouted, and started running across to the hospital. But the scene that met me there was a mirror of that in our own lab, and the one I'd been dreading. There were bodies everywhere, but, instead of vibrant thirty year-old planetary pioneers, we found desiccated shells, shadows of the people they had once been. Kelley lay across the doorway, as if she'd been trying to protect her charges; her peachy skin turned to parchment and her auburn hair turned to straw.

Overcome by thoughts of what might have been, I staggered from the doorway, and nearly crashed into Dina.

She put an arm around me. "Is it...?"

I nodded. I couldn't speak.

She drew me over towards Command. "We need to talk to Luc."

———

But of course, the same sight met us in Command, and in every other module. Ruination and silence. Necrosis and annihilation.

Not one single colonist had survived the night, save for Dina and me. With almost four hundred dead in just twelve hours, our campsite resembled a battlefield more than an expeditionary settlement.

Standing in the centre, I was thinking black thoughts when Dina grabbed my arm.

"Listen!" she said, and I heard a faint beeping noise coming from Comms.

Was someone else alive after all?

CHAPTER FIVE_

Unfortunately, everything inside comms
was the same as when we'd checked earlier, apart
from a flashing light on the control panel, which
was producing the electronic alert.

With a heavy heart, I picked my way round the
bodies and bent over the screen. *Incoming
message*', it read. I pressed the 'read' button, and a
new message flashed onto the screen: *try salt*'.

Salt? I glanced at Dina, but she looked as
mystified as I felt. Running my fingers through my
hair, I wondered what this cryptic message could
mean. "Let's go ask Colony," I said, and motioned
her to follow me.

———

It felt strange to sit in Luc's chair and speak to Colony. But as the highest-ranking survivor, I realised that I was now the default leader. "Colony, we're the last two left," I explained, "the slugs have killed everyone else. But Earth has suggested trying salt."

"*Processing,*" said Colony, and a spinning icon appeared on the screen. A moment later, it said, "*An old folk remedy. Salt melts slugs.*"

I looked round at Dina and shrugged. "Worth a try?"·

"Anything's worth a try," she said, and we started for the door.

"*Wait!*" commanded Colony, and I turned back.

"Yes?"

"*How did the slugs manage to kill everyone? Were the colonists not sleeping in the modules?*"

"They appear to have eaten through the metal hulls of the modules."

The spinning icon appeared again. "*Send a message to Earth. Tell them that the slugs can eat through glass and metal. Report back to me on the results from using salt.*"

My own spinning icon was doing some

processing. "Uh, yeah," I said, and motioned to Dina to follow me. "Let's go."

———

IGNORING COLONY'S SUGGESTION OF messaging Earth, we spent the next couple of hours hunting through the catering storeroom and gathering all our colony's supplies of salt onto one table in the centre of the kitchen.

Biting her lip, Dina said, "This is all we've got?"

"Maybe Earth thought that we'd find salt on whatever planet we ended up on. But Colony's explorations didn't find any, so," I shrugged, "no salt on this planet, I suppose. Although," I paused whilst I raked my memory for information about salt production, "even if there had been, we'd not be safe to mine it, with these slugs out there."

She nodded. "That's true."

"And there's only so much we could make in the lab—our chemical supplies are limited too." Pulling out a chair for Dina, I sat down heavily. "We should eat something. Then I think we'll need to add the salt to water, to eke it out and make spreading it easier."

———

We didn't dare sleep, that night. We sat back-to-back in the Clean Room, lights blazing, eyes staring, jumping at non-existent sounds, and waiting for the inevitable.

Which never came.

In the hazy light of dawn, we crept out of the lab, unable to believe that we were still alive to do so. The rising sun seemed extra beautiful, holding the promise of another unexpected day of life.

The ring of saline solution that we'd poured around the module had crystallised as it dried into a white circle like a magical faery ring. And it appeared to have worked like a charm. On the outside, there were many black smudges, which seemed to be the melted bodies of slugs that had attempted to cross our barrier.

"It worked!" said Dina, surprise evident in her voice.

"Looks like it," I said.

She sighed. "I wish we'd found that out sooner. We could've saved more people."

I glanced sideways at her. She'd said what I should have been thinking. "Let's go find some breakfast," I said. I needed some time to think about our next move.

CHAPTER SIX_

Looking across the table at Dina, I tried hard not to compare her to Kelley. Unfortunately, the kindest word that could be used to describe her was 'pleasant'. She was unremarkable in just about every way—average mind, average face, average body.

For a moment I wondered why Colony didn't give us all the same education, the same chance to develop our intellect, since it had the same thirty years to train each of us. But then I realised that someone with the brain of a professor would hardly be happy mixing chemicals in a lab. So the AI gave each clone just what he or she needed to be fulfilled—nothing more, nothing less.

I scratched my chin. If we were to make a life

here, *she* would have to become a sort of modern-day Eve, and *I* would have to find her attractive enough—and hope that she, likewise, found me attractive enough—to be able to found a dynasty. Every night we would sleep in fear of our faery ring being traversed by the rapacious aliens of this planet; every day we would wonder how much longer our precious supply of salt could possibly last; and every year that passed would be a year closer to the time when a spaceship might arrive from Earth with the technology to capture our nemesis aliens and turn their acidic slime into some sort of monstrous weapon.

I imagined our future; toddlers playing in the long grass, parents snatching them away from the bogey monsters; sullen teenagers storming into the night, never to be seen again; the day the saline ran out and there was a breach in the salt circle...

Then Dina caught my eye, and I could see from her expression that she had been having similar thoughts. "How soon could Earth get some more salt to us?" she asked. "Or a rescue mission?" she added as an afterthought.

"Let's ask them," I said, jumping up from the table, and grabbing her hand. "There should just be time for an answer before dark tonight."

———

THEIR REPLY ARRIVED JUST AS THE AFTERNOON light started to fade towards evening: *'transporter would take twenty years. What could you offer in return?'*

For a long moment I stared at the black words flickering on the screen, then straightened up and took a deep breath. Turning to Dina, I squared my shoulders and held out my hand.

"Dina, would you like to watch the sunset with me? Shall we go for a walk in the forest?"

———

THE END

———

Based on Hugh Howey's 'Half Way Home'

The tremors started on our way to breakfast one morning. Feeling the first vibration, Mica stopped stock-still and her face lit up. "Earthquake!" she said with a grin. "I didn't know this planet had seismic activity." I could see her geologist instincts coming into play as she crouched down and splayed her fingers on the ground, as if to better feel what was happening under her feet.

But my survival instincts were telling me that standing in the middle of camp gawping at the ground as it bucked and reared under our feet was probably *not* recommended. I grabbed her arm. "C'mon, let's get inside, it's not safe out here."

She looked annoyed and shook off my hand. "Leave me—it's not every day a geologist gets to feel an earthquake first hand. Although," her face clouded and a furrow appeared in her brow as she stared at the more distant earth movements, "I'm not sure it *is* an earthquake—"

"Watch out!" I shouted, and grabbed her arm again, pulling her out of the way just in time, as a bombfruit whistled through the air and smacked into the ground just inches from where she'd been crouching. Another whistle and explosion over to our right had us spinning round, and then it seemed to be raining bombfruit; the sound of the bombardment drowning out any crunching or growling from the earth beneath us.

We started sprinting for the nearest solid object, and arrived at the server module wheezing and gasping for breath, fortunately unharmed but covered in splatters of sticky pulp from the fruit that had detonated beside us. Others were not so lucky. One girl had been hit on the shoulder, her arm hanging uselessly at her side, and a boy at the back of the module was nursing a black eye.

"Where's Julie?" I asked, thinking that our resident nurse would be the best person to help them.

"Hopefully not out there," someone said, nodding at the battlefield scene evident through the module door. *But obviously not here.*

"You don't think an earthquake caused this?" I asked Mica, indicating the carnage outside.

She pursed her lips. "I'm not sure."

"But what else could it be?" None of my training had prepared me for something like this.

Rubbing a thumb along her bottom lip, she looked sideways at me. "That's what I'm wondering."

If you liked this extract, *you can get the short story:*

books2read.com/NobodysHeroHWH

USA Today bestselling author Roz Marshall's first encounter with *Half Way Home* was in 2014, after reading Hugh Howey's *Silo* series (and most of  his other works!). In a fortuitous turn of events, soon afterwards Hugh sponsored a short story competition based on *Half Way Home*, and Roz was a prizewinner with *The Final Solution*.

A software engineer turned ski instructor turned author, Roz loves to write uplifting stories set in her native Scotland (when they're not set in space), with strong heroines and page-turning plot lines. She spends her spare time on horseback exploring the glorious Scottish countryside, or with her hubby and their talkative cat and squirrel-obsessed Jack Russell. ☺

Half Way Home stories

Young Adult Science Fiction set in Hugh Howey's *Half Way Home* universe.

- *Nobody's Hero*

Colony Collapse series:

- *The Final Solution*
- *The Final Countdown*
- *The Final Destination*

The ***Celtic Fey*** series [complete]

Portal Fantasy set in Scotland (and the Faerie Realm):

- *Unicorn Magic*
- *Kelpie Curse*
- *Faerie Quest*
- *The Fey Bard*
- *Wizard's Potion*
- *Merlin's Army*

Secrets in the Snow series [complete]

Women's Fiction / Sweet Sports Romance set in a Scottish ski school:

- *Fear of Falling*
- *My Snowy Valentine*
- *The Racer Trials*
- *Snow Blind*
- *Weathering the Storm*

Scottish stories:

- *Still Waters*

———

WRITING AS R.B. MARSHALL:

The ***Highland Horse Whisperer*** series

Cozy Mystery set in Scotland (and London for the prequel):

- *The Secret Santa Mystery*
- *A Corpse at the Castle*
- *A Right Royal Revenge*

- *A Poisoning at the Pageant*
- *A Heist at Harvest (1 Oct 2023)*
- *A Hitman at the Highland Games (due 2023)*

The **Lady Persephone Victorian Cozy Mysteries**

Historical Cozy Mystery set in 1890s Scotland:

- *Picnics, Peers, and Poison (Aug 2023)*
- *Banquets, Butlers, and Bodies (Sept 2023)*
- *Suppers, Stately Homes, and Spies (Oct 2023)*
- *Dinners, Duchesses, and Danger (Jan 2024)*

Multi-author **Anthologies:**

- *Clues, Christmas Trees and Corpses*
- *Mysteries, Midsummer Sun and Murders*
- *Riddles, Resolutions and Revenge (25 July 2023)*

WRITING AS BELLE MCINNES:

Mary's Ladies series [complete]

Sweet/clean Scottish Historical Romance telling the story of Mary Queen of Scots:

- *A Love Divided*
- *A Love Beyond*
- *A Love Concealed*
- *A Love Departed*

The Macrae Legends series

Clean Scottish Historical Romance telling of the beginnings of Clan Macrae, during the time of William Wallace and Robert the Bruce:

- *For Love or Justice (due 2024)*

The ***Highland Horse Whisperer*** series

Cozy Mystery set in Scotland (and London for the prequel):

- *The Secret Santa Mystery*
- *A Corpse at the Castle*
- *A Right Royal Revenge*
- *A Poisoning at the Pageant*
- *A Heist at Harvest* (1 Oct 2023)
- *A Hitman at the Highland Games* (due 2023)

The ***Lady Persephone Victorian Cozy Mysteries***

Historical Cozy Mystery set in 1890s Scotland:

- *Picnics, Peers, and Poison* (Aug 2023)
- *Banquets, Butlers, and Bodies* (Sept 2023)
- *Suppers, Stately Homes, and Spies* (Oct 2023)

- *Dinners, Duchesses, and Danger* (Jan 2024)

*Multi-author **Anthologies:***

- *Clues, Christmas Trees and Corpses*
- *Mysteries, Midsummer Sun and Murders*
- *Riddles, Resolutions and Revenge (25 July 2023)*

———

WRITING AS BELLE MCINNES_

Mary's Ladies *series* [*complete*]

Sweet/clean Scottish Historical Romance telling the story of Mary Queen of Scots:

- *A Love Divided*
- *A Love Beyond*
- *A Love Concealed*
- *A Love Departed*

The Macrae Legends *series*

Clean Scottish Historical Romance telling of the beginnings of Clan Macrae, during the time of William Wallace and Robert the Bruce:

- *For Love or Justice (due 2024)*

ACKNOWLEDGMENTS_

Thanks to Hugh Howey for his amazing generosity in letting us use our imaginations to play in his fictitious universe.

www.ingramcontent.com/pod-product-compliance
Lightning Source LLC
Chambersburg PA
CBHW021139130726
47988CB00003B/1379